BAD FOOD

The Good, the Bad and the Hungry

By Eric Luper

Illustrated by
"The Doodle Boy" Joe Whale

Scholastic Inc.

© 2022 The Doodle Boy Ltd.

All rights reserved. Published by Scholastic Inc., *Publishers since 1920.* SCHOLASTIC and associated logos are trademarks and/or registered trademarks of Scholastic Inc.

The publisher does not have any control over and does not assume any responsibility for author or third-party websites or their content.

This book is a work of fiction. Names, characters, places, and incidents are either the product of the author's imagination or are used fictitiously, and any resemblance to actual persons, living or dead, business establishments, events, or locales is entirely coincidental.

ISBN 978-1-338-74926-7

2 2022

Printed in the U.S.A.   23

First printing 2022

Book design by Katie Fitch

SCHOOL MAP

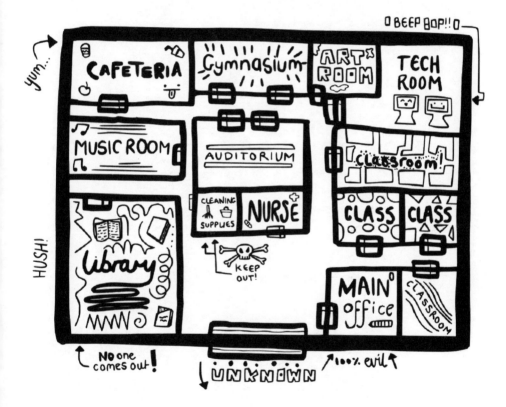

CHAPTER 1

Where We Begin All Over Again

It was an average night at Belching Walrus Elementary. The doors were locked, the hallways were quiet, and the moon and stars shone brightly through the high windows. Oh, and also all the food in the Cafeteria was jamming out.

HEY MAN!!

No, what I meant to say is that the food in the Cafeteria at

Belching Walrus Elementary actually comes alive each night to party. Every night.

And ever since the folks from the other rooms in the school helped stop Baron von Lineal's evil plans . . .

Okay, what I meant to say is ever since the folks from the other rooms at Belching Walrus Elementary helped stop Baron von Lineal's *misguided* plans, they've been coming to the Cafeteria each night to hang out as well.

I OBJECT!

THEY WERE MISGUIDED PLANS, NOT EVIL ONES!

And, as always, our favorite foodie friends—Slice (a brave slice of pizza), Scoop (a triple scoop ice cream cone—vanilla, chocolate, AND strawberry), and Totz (a crunchy, delicious, and trendy tater tot)—were doing their own thing under the utility sink.

Of course, their new friends came around often to say "Wassup."

Before we go on too long, it might be a good idea to meet some of our new friends. After all, if you

don't like these new friends, you might decide to put this book down and do something completely differ-

ent. Maybe you'd prefer to swim in a pool filled with chocolate pudding? Or drink a big glass of warm prune juice? Maybe you'd rather be buried under a pile of chubby, yapping puppies? So, here goes:

Ducky

Type: Brass paperweight

Job: Sitting on papers (it sounds boring, but someone has to hold papers down!)

Personality: The strong, silent type

Strengths: Weightiness, strong sense of right and wrong

Weaknesses: Slow, a little clumsy, waddles

Hobbies: What's more fun than sitting on papers?

Catchphrase: None. Does not speak.

Sal

Type: An Egg

Flavor: Eggy protein with a hint of cholesterol, maybe a bit saltier than Monella

Personality: Cheery, organized, energetic

Strengths: Protective of Monella

Weaknesses: Fragile (almost like an egg!)

Wobble Factor: High

Hobbies: Speed walking, but dancing is his secret talent. Shhh . . .

Monella

Type: Also an Egg

Flavor: Also eggy protein with a hint of cholesterol

Personality: Brave but maybe a bit reckless

Strengths: Protective of the Pantry

Weaknesses: Also fragile (almost like an egg!)

Wobble Factor: Even higher

Hobbies: Speed walking

BLU1 and GRN1

Type: Drones

Job: Completing directives

Strengths: Flying, zippiness, no fear

Weaknesses: Limited battery life, no sense of humor, noisy

Hobbies: "Hobbies do not compute."

Catchphrase: "Beep, bop, boop."

Just like in your own school cafeteria, there are plenty of other yummy folks bouncing around, but you'll meet them as the story goes on (unless you stopped reading a few pages ago and are currently searching for a pool filled with chocolate pudding or a pile of chubby, yapping puppies). No matter, we're going to forge ahead with our story about Belching Walrus Elementary. So, if you dare (and if you aren't thirsty for some warm prune juice), read on.

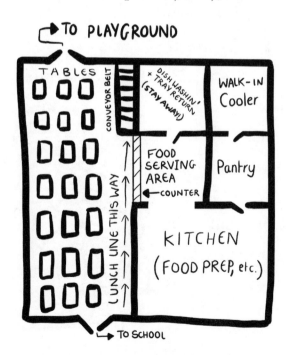

CHAPTER 2

Heels Over Head

Hey, Totz," **Scoop said.** "Have you written any new rhymes?"

"Not lately," Totz said. "I'm working on a *new* project."

"What's your new project?" Slice asked.

Totz adjusted his

sunglasses and tucked his tiny pad into his pocket. "What is your greatest fear?" he asked.

"Melting," Scoop said. "Being dropped on a hot summer sidewalk and melting—little chocolate, vanilla, and strawberry rivers trickling into a puddle. I shiver just thinking about it."

Slice looked over his shoulder at the huge gaping jaws at the end of a conveyor belt. "For me, it's going in there," he said. "The dishwasher."

"Exactly," Totz  said. "Food goes in, but it never comes out."

"I've heard that before," Scoop said.

"It all started not long after I came out of the box," Totz explained. "I was walking along and . . ."

I was walking along, minding my own business . . .

But the conveyor belt was moving too fast. There was nothing I could do.

The plate was clean—horribly and disgustingly clean.

13

"That moment, I vowed to someday defeat my fears..." Totz said. "And defeat the dishwasher."

"How are you going to do that?" Scoop asked.

"I found the plans for the dishwasher," Totz said. "I'm going to figure out how to get through. To survive the Wash Cycle, I'll have to dodge, flip, and spin three times. To beat the Rinse Cycle, I'll have to slide, jump, and do the limbo two times. To defeat the Dry Cycle, I'll need to shimmy, shake, and do the Worm once."

"Is that all?" Slice said. "Sounds so easy."

"That's *not* all," Totz said ominously. "To get through the Plate-Stacking Cycle, I'll have to do one cartwheel."

"A cartwheel?!" Scoop said. "My mom told me if I do a cartwheel my ice cream will plop right out of my cone."

Ducky's eyes got wide.

"Tater tots don't have that problem," Totz said.

He flipped through his notepad. "I just need to learn how to do that cartwheel, and I'll overcome my biggest fear."

Slice looked Totz over. "I'm not sure your arms are long enough to do a cartwheel."

"There's only one way to find out." Totz took a deep breath, kicked up one leg, and threw himself sideways. Headphones flew in one direction. Sunglasses flew in another. A few crumbs ended up on the tile floor. And Totz found himself flat on his crunchy back.

"I'd say that needs some work," Slice said.

Ducky nodded.

"Keep practicing," Scoop said. "You'll get it right."

"Or I'll end up hash browns," Totz said, gathering his things.

"I've never met a hash brown I didn't like," Slice said.

Just then, Sal and Monella came running up. Their cheeks glowed pink as they tried to catch their breath.

"Hey, y'all." Sal panted. "We have something to show you."

"Is it directions on how to do a cartwheel?" Totz asked. "I could use some help."

"No, it's a poster," Monella said, her hands on her hips.

"Is it a poster with a kitten on it that says *Sharing Is Caring*?" Scoop asked. "That poster got us in a lot of trouble back when Baron von Lineal showed up."

"No," Sal said. "It says something about limping. And games."

For further information about kittens on posters, please read our first book *Game of Scones*.

"Games?" Slice asked.

"Limping?" Scoop added.

"Or lamps," Monella said. "Maybe it was lamps."

"Limping lamps maybe . . . ? We're not very good

at reading," Sal said. "Come with us. We'll show you."

As the gang headed from the Kitchen into the Cafeteria, Sal and Monella explained.

"We were out on our daily speed walk when we saw the poster," Monella said.

"It was stuck right up there on the wall between the water fountain and the window," Sal said.

"Sort of a dark corner," Monella said. "I'm surprised we saw it at all."

"What's speed walking?" Slice asked.

"It's a sport where you walk as fast as you can," Monella said.

Sal nodded. "You have to have at least one foot on the ground at all times, and your front leg needs to be straight when it hits the ground."

"Your leg also needs to be straight when it passes under your body," Monella added.

"Sounds complicated," Totz said. "Why don't you just run? That's what Slice and I do when we're being chased by angry mops or a mob of angry library books."

"Because then it's not speed walking, silly," Monella said.

"It looks like this," Sal said.

Sal started speed-walking across the floor. His eggy hips swung back and forth in a strange figure-eight pattern as he sped ahead of them all.

"Wait for me!" Monella called out as she started speed-walking after him.

Ducky tried to speed-*waddle* for a few paces but quickly gave up.

"I'm not sure you're built for speed walking, Ducky," Scoop said. "You can get around normally like the rest of us."

By the time Slice, Scoop, Totz, and Ducky got to the water fountain, Sal and Monella were already there. Their cheeks were pink, just like before.

Something out the window caught Scoop's eye. A tiny light blinked in the sky. Red . . . blue . . . green . . . yellow . . . red . . . blue . . . green . . . yellow . . . The light zipped to the left, then zipped to the right. Then it disappeared.

"What's wrong?" Totz asked Scoop.

"Nothing," she said. "It must have been a little ice cream in my eyes."

"See? Right there." Sal panted. "The poster we told you about."

They all crowded around to see what it said.

"What could it mean?" Sal asked.

Slice read it a second time. "Well, clearly, it's an Interdepartmental, Interdisciplinary, Intergalactic Olympic Games," he said, sounding just as confused as everyone else felt.

Scoop sighed. "Sometimes, I just wish Richard the dictionary was around to tell us what words mean."

"No!!!" Slice and Totz said at once. Even Ducky shook his head violently.

Richard was a huge blue dictionary who lived in the Library. Not only was Richard always grouchy, but he once jumped off a high shelf and tried to squash Slice and Totz. They barely survived!

"Good point," Scoop said. A long drip of vanilla trickled past her left eye. "But we'd better figure out what this is quick. It's supposed to happen right here in the Cafeteria."

"You'd better get back to the Cooler," Slice said to Scoop. "You're dripping everywhere!"

CHAPTER 3

Interdepartmental, Interdis—All That Stuff

I wonder when those posters went up," Slice said as they rushed back to the Pantry.

"What does it matter?" Sal asked.

Slice thought it through for a moment. "Well, if the posters were put up today, the Olympics would be in two days."

Sal nodded. "That's exactly what the poster says."

"But if they were put up yesterday . . ."

"Then the Olympics would be tomorrow," Scoop said, wiping a few strawberry drips from her forehead.

Ducky opened the Cooler door, and Scoop took a deep breath of the chilled air. She seemed to perk up instantly.

Totz glanced at Slice with worry, then turned to Sal and Monella. "When was the first time you remember seeing those posters?" he asked them.

Sal and Monella looked at each other.

"Uh . . . we don't pay much attention to the walls," Sal said.

"Yeah, we only focus on having the speediest speed walk we can," Monella said.

Scoop caught on to what Slice and Totz were thinking. "So, if the posters were put up *two* days ago, then the Interdisciplinary, Interoffice, Intergalactic Olympics . . ."

"Would be TODAY!!!" a voice exclaimed.

They all turned to see who just spoke.

It was Baron von Lineal. He stood there with a tiny clipboard in his hands. Two staplers were lined up behind him.

"I hope you have prepared for all the fun events I have in store for you and the rest of Belching

Walrus Elementary," Lineal announced. "There will be running and jumping and swimming and flipping and ballroom dancing and much, much more."

"Will there be slam dunking?" asked a pine-apple, who was standing nearby. "I love slam dunking."

"There will be no slam dunking," Baron von Lineal announced.

"THERE WILL BE NO SLAM DUNKING!" both staplers repeated.

"I'm pretty sure we're okay with not being in your Olympics," Slice said.

"Nonsense," Baron von Lineal said. "Everyone will love my Olympics."

"But it wasn't too long ago that you tried to take over our Cooler," Totz said. "Why would we trust you now?"

Baron von Lineal laughed. "We've all made mistakes in the past," he said. "Consider the Olympics my way of saying *I'm sorry* to you and all the residents of the Cafeteria."

"So, what does 'interdepartmental' mean?" Scoop asked.

Baron von Lineal turned to the stapler to his left.

"*INTERDEPARTMENTAL* MEANS EACH GROUP WILL ACT AS A TEAM!" the stapler hollered.

"What does 'interdisciplinary' mean?" Totz asked.

Baron von Lineal turned to the stapler to his right.

"*INTERDISCIPLINARY* MEANS THERE WILL BE MANY EVENTS SO EACH ROOM IN THE SCHOOL WILL HAVE A CHANCE TO SHINE," the second stapler said.

"And 'intergalactic'?" Slice asked. "What does that mean?"

Both staplers barked at once: "*INTERGALACTIC* MEANS ALL ARE INVITED!"

Ducky's wings fluttered, and he shrunk back. He clearly did not trust Baron von Lineal and his goons.

"I'm not so sure this is a good idea," Slice said. "We're going to have to talk it over with Glizzy, Sprinkles, and the rest of the Cafeteria."

Baron von Lineal looked down at his clipboard. "But we have Totz scheduled to perform at the opening ceremonies."

Everyone looked at Totz.

"No one told me," Totz said.

"We'd still like to discuss it with the rest of the Cafeteria," Slice said.

"Talk about it all you like," Lineal said. "But don't take too long. The Interdepartmental, Interdisciplinary, Intergalactic Olympics begins in nine minutes."

"Nine minutes?!?" Slice, Scoop, Totz, Sal, and Monella said at once. If Ducky could speak, he surely would have said *Nine minutes?!?*

"But of course . . . The posters have been up for one day, twenty-three hours, and fifty-one minutes. Only nine minutes left. It's not my fault none of you stopped to read something we put up in a dark corner between the water fountain and the windows."

"Wait, you didn't want us to see that poster," Slice said.

"You didn't want us to be ready for your games!" Totz accused.

"Don't be silly," Baron von Lineal said. "These games are meant to bring everyone at Belching Walrus Elementary together, not to have the Main Office win every event, every medal, every honor, every accolade, and every award."

"Is an accolade a French dessert?" Sal whispered. "I love French desserts."

"An accolade is *not* a French dessert!" Baron von Lineal snapped. "It is an honor given to someone for performing a great deed."

"And the great deed in this case would be beating the Cafeteria in every event?" Scoop asked.

Baron von Lineal smiled. "These games will be FUN AND FAIR," he said. "In fact, there will be a judge from every room in the school. Anyhow, we just spoke to Glizzy, and he agreed."

"It's true." They turned to see Glizzy step out of the darkness of a high shelf.

"I sent BLU1 and GRN1 to the four corners of the school to ask around," he said. "Everyone will be participating

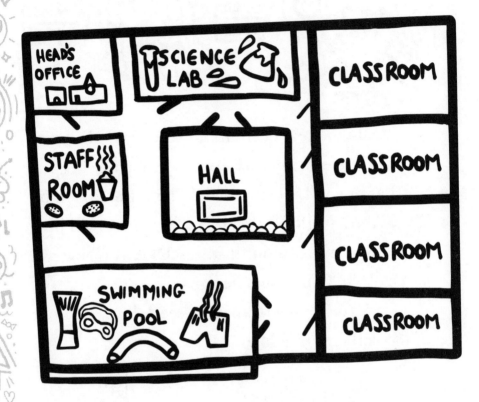

HEAD'S OFFICE

SCIENCE LAB

CLASSROOM

STAFF ROOM

HALL

CLASSROOM

CLASSROOM

SWIMMING POOL

CLASSROOM

in the Interdepartmental, Interdisciplinary, Intergalactic Olympic Games."

Coach from the Gym said, "We're in!"

François from the Art Room said, "We'd be tickled pink!"

Baton from the Music Room said, "We shall compose the theme song!"

Spex with Richard from the Library said, "We will be there."

"But, Glizzy," Slice said. "Baron von Lineal—"

"Baron von Lineal made some mistakes," Glizzy said. "But everyone deserves a second chance. Plus, we are hosting the games. It is a great honor."

"Is it an accolade?" Totz asked.

"Not an accolade," Baron von Lineal said. "An honor. There is a difference."

"We will win the accolade for speed walking," Monella said.

Baron von Lineal looked down at tiny Monella.

"There will be no speed walking in my Olympics, little egg. Speed walking is not a serious sport." He clapped his hands twice. "Now, CHOP, CHOP! It's nearly time for the opening ceremonies!"

But Slice, Scoop, and Totz felt uneasy. For one, no food likes hearing the word *chop*.

And second, they knew Baron von Lineal must have something up his sleeve.

CHAPTER 4

Opening Ceremonies

Before long, the Cafeteria was filled with folks from all over Belching Walrus Elementary. The instruments from the Music Room began playing a grand song. The athletes marched down a long aisle between the Cafeteria tables.

Slice, Totz, and Scoop worked their way to the front of the crowd just in time to see Baron von Lineal and his friends from the Main Office march past. That group was followed by Coach and the folks from the Gym. Then came François and the Art Room, Baton and the rest of the instruments, and Spex Bifocals and the Library. One by one, the groups passed by.

"So, what do you think Baron von Lineal's plan is?" Slice asked.

"Who knows?" Totz said. "Maybe he's turned over a new leaf."

"He's a gardener now?" Slice asked.

"Totz just means that maybe Lineal is trying to do something nice," Scoop said.

"Why is it nice to turn over a leaf?" Slice asked.

BLU1, GRN1, and a few other drones from the Tech Room swooped past.

"Maybe he is turning over a new leaf," Slice

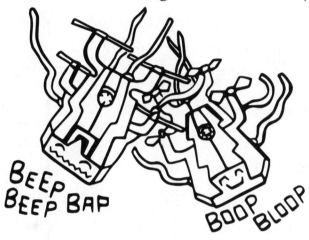

said. "This ceremony sure is nice. But keep your eyes open. Stay on alert."

When the parade was over, Baron von Lineal

climbed onto a milk crate and faced the crowd. Everyone grew silent, and he cleared his throat. "Ladies and gentlemen, pens and pencils, dictionaries, oboes, basketballs, meat loaves, computer mice *(or is that 'mouses'?)*, paintbrushes, high-

lighters, hockey sticks, pineapples, atlases, chocolate chip cookies . . . er . . . all of you . . . welcome to the first Interdepartmental, Interdisciplinary, Intergalactic Olympic Games. We have many exciting events and activities planned for you. Each room in Belching Walrus Elementary, please ask your best athletes to participate, and let the competition begin!"

Just then, a tiny paper clip ran into the Cafeteria and down the aisle. She hopped onto a box and struggled up the leg of a chair. Then she leaped to the countertop and pulled herself up. She jogged across to the stove and with great effort turned one of the dials. A tiny blue flame poofed on.

Everyone cheered.

"I've never seen anything so beautiful," one chicken nug said.

"Stunning!" a tennis ball cried out.

"More inspiring than a mountain of glitter glue and sparkle pens," François the paintbrush said, wiping a tear from his eye.

Baron von Lineal cleared his throat. "But before

DON'T PLAY WITH FIRE, YOU'LL MELT!

HIIISSSS

we begin our first competition, I'd like to invite Totz of the Cafeteria up here to set the mood."

A drum started beating, and a calculator started blinking.

"You all remember Totz, right?" Baron von Lineal said. "He's the Master of Rhymes, the Sultan of Some Stuff, the Deacon of . . . well, you know."

The crowd roared. Celery cheered. Balls bounced in excitement. Drones buzzed their approval.

Totz looked concerned. He hadn't had time to prepare. But he walked to the stage, anyway. He started pacing back and forth to the beat. Slice and Scoop could see he was trying to work out some good rhymes.

Finally, he came out with it:

"We've all come together to celebrate with games.
So many folks here, it drives me insane.
But before we break up and start to compete,
Stay right there for my ultra-wicked beat.

Tech Room, Gym, and Musical dudes.
Library, Office, all kinds of food.
I see some folks I don't even know.
But I'll keep shaking hands so my friend list can grow.

Interdepartmental—
All rooms can play.
Interdisciplinary—
Games all the day.
Intergalactic—
From far and wide.
So, strap on your sneakers.
Compete for Room Pride.

Running, jumping, the flippiest flip.
Better slow down or your pants will rip.
So, get on now before this train has departed.
But hold on to your hat cuz we're just getting started!"

Everyone went wild—cheering, clapping hands, stomping feet, and throwing confetti. When they settled down, Baron von Lineal looked out at the crowd.

"Let the games begin!"

Just then, the window near the water fountain flung open. Wind gusted in, flapping the heavy curtains, and a large silver disk floated into the Cafeteria. It made a pulsing, humming sort of sound and blinked different color lights. Red . . . blue . . . green . . . yellow . . . red . . . blue . . . green . . . yellow . . . Intense white spotlights scanned the room.

Finally, the disc lowered onto a table, and white steam puffed out from the sides. A ramp lowered, and out walked two creatures that looked unlike anything anyone at Belching Walrus Elementary had ever seen.

One creature had a long neck and small eyes. The other creature had a short neck and small eyes. They both wore tank tops that said xyzyx across the chest. And instead of feet, they sat atop a nest of tentacles.

The creature with the long neck and the small eyes waved. "Hey there, everyone," he said. "I am Gleb. I am from the planet Xyzyx. And this here is my friend, Lauren. Thank you for your invitation. We'd love to participate in your Olympic Games."

CHAPTER 5

Where Someone Says, "Now, Wait a Second Here"

Now, wait a second here," Baron von Lineal said. "These Olympic Games are only open to the folks at Belching Walrus Elementary. That's why we called it *Interdepartmental*."

Gleb smiled (at least Slice thought it was a smile). "It is my understanding that Interdepartmental means each group will act as a team. Why can't Lauren and I be our own team?"

Lauren nodded in agreement and cheerfully said, "Squ@rk!!"

A murmur spread through the Cafeteria.

Gleb walked to the edge of the table. The glow from his spaceship lit him up. "Anyhow, what about Intergalactic? Your poster also mentions Intergalactic... and we're from another galaxy."

Folks murmured more.

"In fact, without us, your games wouldn't be

Intergalactic at all," Gleb said. "They would just be Inter-Room. That's not very fancy, is it?"

Lauren nodded in agreement and said, "Squ@rk!!"

"Where did you hear about our Olympic Games?" Baron von Lineal asked. "I don't remember inviting you."

"We found out about it through radio transmission," Gleb explained. "We constantly scan the universe for games to compete in. When you printed out your posters, we just happened to be finishing a pickle-eating contest on Pluto and came across your kind invitation. We can monitor anything that goes over your Wi-Fi."

WHY US? OUT OF THIS WORLD!!!! BARBARIANS!! CRUEL! OFFENSIVE! CHEEKY!! THEY'VE GOT TO GO! DEMONS! WEIRDOS! WELL, I NEVER!

"Squ@rk!" Lauren said.

"Exactly," Gleb said.

Totz leaned over to Scoop. "What does Squ@rk mean?"

"I have no idea," she replied.

Baron von Lineal looked to Chip from the Tech Room.

Chip shrugged. `"It is possible they intercepted our signal."`

"Why wouldn't we want our new friends from Xyzyx to compete in our games?" Glizzy said. "I say let them play."

Slice agreed. He started chanting, "Let them play . . . Let them play . . ."

Folks started joining in.

"Let . . . them . . . play . . ."

"Let . . . them . . . play . . ."

Before long, even more folks were chanting.

"LET THEM PLAY!!!"

"LET THEM PLAY!!!"

Baron von Lineal opened his mouth to protest.

But then he thought about it for a moment. Then he opened his mouth again to protest. But thought about it a few seconds longer. Then he sighed. "I suppose we have no choice," he said.

"It's not that we have no choice," Coach said. "We WANT them to play. The more competition the better!"

A cheer rose up among the folks at Belching Walrus Elementary. After all, it wasn't every day that an alien spacecraft flew in through the window and insisted on competing against you in Olympic Games.

Once everyone settled down, Baron von Lineal got back to business. "The first game in our Olympics will be a footrace around the school. There is a walkway around the entire building. We will open the doors, and the first one to run all the way around Belching Walrus Elementary and return here wins. Please bring forward your fastest feet and get ready to use them!"

Before long, folks from each room started lining up near the door.

Tennis Ball, the Gym

Rubber Band, the Main Office

Bottle of Glue, the Art Room

Xylophone, the Music Room

GRNI (drone), the Tech Room

Spex Bifocals, the Library

Lauren, Planet Xyzyx

Everyone from the Cafeteria circled around.

"I'd run this race," Glizzy said, "but I've been out there. It was at the Great School Cookout. Many of us went; few returned. They called us Leftovers after that. I swore I'd never go back."

"So, who's going to run the race?" Sprinkles the Donut asked.

"I'll melt," Ice Cube said.

"I'll squish," Stick of Butter complained.

"What if I spill?" Glass of Milk worried.

"I'll do it," Pineapple said. "I mean, I'd rather be slam dunking, but this sounds fun, too."

There was a long pause. There was no way Pineapple was fast enough to win a footrace around the school. In fact, no one had ever seen Pineapple move faster than a drip of maple syrup in the wintertime.

"Ummm, why don't you save your energy for another sport?" Glizzy said. "Slice, how about you?"

"Me?" Slice said. "I'm no runner."

"Nonsense," Glizzy said. "You ran away from the mops in the hallway. You ran away from falling books in the Library. You ran away from Baron von Lineal in the—"

"You make it sound like all I do is run away," Slice said.

"So, it's settled," Sprinkles said. "Slice will run in the first sport in the Interdepartmental, Interdisciplinary, Intergalactic Olympic Games."

CHAPTER 6

On Your Marks . . . Get Set . . .

I've never run this far before," Slice said. "Plus, GRN1 is a drone. They fly at like a million miles an hour. How am I supposed to beat a drone?"

Totz patted Slice on the shoulder. "You've got this," he said. "Just think of a beat in your head and run to that beat."

"I don't have any beats in my head," Slice said.

"How about this?" Totz said.

His head started bopping to the beat and he came out with some lyrics:

"One step, two steps, three steps, more.
Some think running is a bore.
I'll stay ahead and set the pace.
Watch out, world—I'll win this race!"

"Uh, yeah," Slice said. "There's no way I'll remember that. I only run fast if I'm running for my life."

"Then imagine a giant pizza cutter chasing you," Scoop suggested.

The thought sent shivers down Slice's crust.

"Just run the best race you can for *you*," Scoop said. "That's all anyone can expect."

"I'll do my best," Slice said.

The athletes lined up while Ducky, Apple, Bass Drum, and Richard the dictionary pushed at the door. Even though they were the strongest folks at Belching Walrus Elementary, they still struggled to open it.

It was dark outside. Streetlights glowed, creating white circles on the sidewalk as it stretched along the side of the school. Wind swirled dead leaves into the air. A crow cawed in the distance.

Xylophone played a creepy tune.

"Ladies and gentlemen!" Baron von Lineal announced. "The first event of our Olympics is about to begin!"

"Squ@rk!" Lauren belted out.

Baron von Lineal gave Lauren a slightly annoyed look. "After discussing the matter with our judges, we

have decided that one of our athletes has been disqualified from the footrace."

A buzz spread throughout the crowd. The athletes started looking back and forth at one another. Lauren said, "Squ@rk!"

"The judges have decided that GRN1 is not allowed to run in the footrace," Lineal said. "This decision was not an easy one, but it seems unfair to allow GRN1 to run a race when drones do not run at all. Drones fly. As such, the Tech Room has been disqualified from this event."

GRN1's propellers whirred, and it floated into the air. "This is a fair and just decision," GRN1 said. "I will stand aside and let those with feet run with their feet."

FAIR = FAIR

"Now, please line up," Lineal said to the athletes. They all lined up at the doorway.

Slice looked to his left. Bottle of Glue said, "Bottles of glue are *not* known for their running abilities."

Slice looked to his right. Rubber Band had hooked herself on the edge of the door and stretched back. "All stretched out and ready to snap!" she said.

Lauren stood at the end of the row. Gleb gave her a spoonful of glistening yellow goop. Her long, eely tongue slithered across her lips, and she swallowed. "Squ@rk!" she said.

"On your marks!" Baron von Lineal said. "Get set . . . GO!!!"

A cymbal crashed, and all the athletes started running.

Slice tried to remember the words to the poem Totz had given him:

"One step, two paces, three lunges, four?
Uh . . . a bunch of words that I ignored.
Running really makes my legs ache.
But I'll keep on running because I can't rhyme."

Tennis Ball got an early lead, bouncing along the sidewalk like a ball, which made sense because he was a ball. Xylophone had wheels, but she was slower than Slice had expected, due to the rough concrete. Bottle of Glue was slow, too. But that was no surprise. She was a bottle of glue. Suddenly, Rubber Band snapped past into the lead with Lauren not far behind.

"Squ@rk!" Lauren said.

Slice knew not to worry about everyone else and to run his *own best race*, just like Scoop had told him. He first imagined a giant pizza cutter chasing him, but that was too scary a thought. He then thought about happier things like sausage and mushroom toppings and extra cheese. This brought a smile to his exhausted face and allowed him to forget how badly his legs ached.

Something fluttered in a bush to their right. Slice ignored it and kept running.

Run your own best race . . . Run your own best race . . . Run your own best race . . . Scoop's words echoed in his head.

Something fluttered in the creepy branches above them.

Slice kept running. The group turned the corner and kept going. Belching Walrus Elementary was way bigger on the outside than it seemed on the inside. And it seemed BIG on the inside! They turned another corner.

Something fluttered in the branches again.

"Caw!"

A crow swooped down and plucked Slice right off the sidewalk.

"Heeelp!" he screamed.

As they flew into the air, the sidewalk grew farther away. Slice could see sports fields, a playground, and a parking lot. It might have been interesting if he wasn't so filled with terror. Now he knew why Glizzy never wanted to go outside again. The crow's sharp talons dug into Slice's soft cheese. He struggled. He twisted. He strained. He thrashed. It worked!

The crow swooped down again to grab Slice. "Caw!" it cawed again.

Suddenly . . . *Pok!*

Tennis Ball hit the crow in the wing. The bird fluttered back.

Snap! Rubber Band hit the bird, too.

Glug, glug, glug . . . and Bottle of Glue got the bird's feathers sticky.

Xylophone rolled up and played a loud, creepy song.

The crow fluttered back and flew away to the nearest branch.

"Hey, thanks, y'all." Slice panted. "That was a close call."

"That's how we roll," Tennis Ball said.

"Yeah," Rubber Band added. "Baron von Lineal said the games were meant to bring us all together."

"We couldn't just leave you out here to be street food," Xylophone said.

Slice stood up and dusted himself off. "I guess we should finish this race, huh?"

"That's what we're here for," Bottle of Glue said as he trotted off along the sidewalk.

By the time they rounded the last corner of the school, Lauren had already crossed the finish line. Gleb danced around her, their tentacles in the air. Still, the glow from the doorway to the Cafeteria made Slice want to run faster. Not only did it mean he could go back inside to the safety of the Cafeteria, but he still had a chance to take second place.

The glow of the doorway grew larger. The cheers of the spectators grew louder. The hammering in his chest grew more hammery. Slice gave everything he had.

Just as he was about to cross the finish line, Tennis Ball bounced past to earn second place. "Game, set, and match!" he said.

Slice tumbled forward and flopped onto his belly to take third. The rest of the athletes crossed soon after.

Slice was glad to be done. He had run his own best race, but he still felt disappointed. He rolled onto his back to see Scoop and Totz looking down at him.

"That was . . . AWESOME!" Totz said.

"So amazing!" Scoop cried out.

They picked Slice up and led him to the podium to receive his medal.

CHAPTER 7

The Games Continue

After they gave medals to the winners of the foot-race, Baron von Lineal announced the next competitions . . .

Tennis
(Lauren won.)

Figure Skating
(Lauren won.)

Rhythmic
Gymnastics
(Lauren won.)

Trampoline
(Lauren won.)

"It looks like Lauren is going to win every event in the Interdepartmental, Interdisciplinary, Intergalactic Olympic Games," Slice said. "We've been giving it everything we've got, and no one has even come close."

"Don't give up hope yet," Totz said, patting Slice on the shoulder. "That alien can't be good at *everything*."

But she was. Lauren kept winning event after event after event after event after event. Swimming. Golf. Parkour. Cheese rolling.

CHEESE ROLLING IS CRUEL!

Unicycle polo. Full-contact ironing. Moonwalking. Jumping over shoeboxes while wearing a blindfold with one hand tied to your opposite foot.

I TRIED TO MAKE UP A FEW SPORTS THAT WE MIGHT WIN...

As Scoop strapped on her tiny snowboard for the next event, Slice and Totz gathered around to talk.

"Something seems fishy," Totz said.

"That might be my anchovies," Slice admitted.

"Not that," Scoop said. "Have you noticed that Gleb feeds Lauren a spoonful of something before every event?"

"It's some sort of glistening yellow goop," Totz said. "What could it be?"

"Totz and I will keep an eye on Gleb while you win a medal for the Cafeteria," Slice said.

They looked up at the mountain of shaved ice spilling out of the Cooler. Baron von Lineal stood at the top.

"We have spared no expense to bring you the finest in sports for our Interdepartmental, Interdisciplinary—and yes—Intergalactic Olympic Games," Lineal said. "This may be our crowning achievement—a ski mountain!"

Everyone cheered.

It *was* an impressive ski mountain. It had a few different slopes, a long, narrow chute for bobsledding, and a U-shaped half-pipe for Scoop's favorite sport.

MY FAVORITE SPORTS ARE WINTER SPORTS.

As the athletes started climbing to the top of the icy mountain, Scoop and Totz looked around for Gleb.

"He's not in the main part of the Cafeteria," Totz said.

"He's not in the Kitchen," Slice said.

"He's not in the Cooler," Totz said. "Maybe he's in the Pantry."

As they snuck around the corner into the Pantry, they heard a noise.

"Please be quiet," a voice said. "This will all be over soon."

Slice and Totz hid behind a box of oatmeal to see what was going on. It was Gleb. He was climbing out of a cardboard box, a tiny spoon clutched in one hand. The spoon was filled with a scoop of glistening yellow goop.

"We don't want it to be over," a tiny voice said.

"Now, hush," the first voice said. "Who doesn't want to go up into space and see the stars?"

Gleb slithered out of the Pantry with his spoon. Slice and Totz crept over to see what was going on. Gleb had just been in a huge box of mustard packets!

"Thank goodness you've come," one mustard packet said. "Gleb and Lauren are eating us one at a time. Mustard gives them superstrength, superspeed, and superstamina. Plus, it powers their ship."

"Poor Dijon," another mustard packet moaned.

"They plan to take us to planet Xyzyz and eat us all!" another mustard packet said. (Or was it that first one? No one could tell since every mustard packet looks exactly the same and every mustard packet's voice sounds exactly the same. They even use the same toothpaste.)

"So, Gleb and Lauren have been cheating this whole time," Slice said. "So much for *fair and fun games.*"

"Uh, plus they've been EATING US," another mustard packet said.

WE ALSO BRUSH OUR TEETH

WE'RE FILLED WITH GLUCOSINOLATESSS!!

"We have to stop them," Totz insisted. "They can't win *all* the medals."

"And that part about eating us," another mustard packet said.

"You all wait here," Slice said. "We'll see what we can do."

Slice and Totz returned to the Cooler just in time to see the end of Scoop's snowboarding run. She did an inverted handplant into a triple McTwist, finishing with a quadruple Haakon flip.

Everyone cheered for Scoop while Lauren strapped on her snowboard at the top of the ski mountain. The judges held up their scores.

"Almost a perfect score!" Slice said.

But Lauren had already started down the half-pipe. The tricks she performed no one could describe. They were the flippiest, twistiest, spinniest tricks anyone had ever seen. And just when folks thought they had seen something amazing, Lauren topped it by doing something even more amazing.

As she glided past at the end of her run, Slice could see a drip of mustard on her lips. Her eely tongue slurped it up.

"We've got to stop them," Totz said.

CHAPTER 8
Yellow Is Yellow Is Yellow?

I **don't know** what to do," Baron von Lineal said to Glizzy. "I wanted to have a fair and fun Olympic Games, but Gleb and Lauren have ruined it all."

Glizzy stroked his handlebar mustache as he thought about it.

"You didn't want these games to be fair and fun at all," Slice said.

"What are you suggesting?" Baron von Lineal scoffed.

"You put up posters in places that no one would notice," Totz said.

"And we only had nine minutes to prepare," Scoop added.

"Now that I think about it," Glizzy said, "it seems that you wanted the Main Office to win every event."

Baron von Lineal straightened. "Of course I did," he said. "I have great pride in the athletic talents of the Main Office. Our staplers are the strongest. Our highlighters are the brightest. Our paper clips are the twistiest. But this is unfair."

"I think I might know how to stop them," Slice said. "But you're going to have to trust us."

"Done," Baron von Lineal said.

"Plus, we want something in return," Scoop added.

"Name it . . ." Lineal said.

Slice, Totz, and Scoop rushed from classroom to classroom. Not only did the next event start in a few minutes, but they also needed to get a lot done before Scoop started melting. They started with the Art Room to gather a few things, then ran to the Main Office. From there, they darted to the Music Room for an item or two, and then to the Gym.

As they headed back down the hallway, Slice paused.

"Our final stop is going to be dangerous," he said.

They looked up at a huge wooden door. A brass plate in the center read CUSTODIAN CLOSET.

"We c-c-can't . . ." Totz stuttered. "You know what happened last time."

Slice *did* know what happened last time. In fact, every night since the cleaning supplies burst out of the closet and chased them down the hallway, he had been having nightmares about it. Even though Glizzy

turned out okay, Slice couldn't get the image of him being whomped by a mop out of his mind.

"We have no choice," Slice said.

"But Glizzy told us they are nothing more than mindless beasts," Scoop said.

Slice knocked on the door.

No answer.

He knocked again.

The door slowly creaked open. The closet was dark. They peered in more closely.

Something stirred.

"Who dares disturb the slumber of the Belching Walrus Elementary cleaning supplies?" a gravelly voice rasped.

"We ... uh ... we come from the Cafeteria," Slice said. "We have been very tidy lately. And we need to ask a favor."

There was a long pause, and then movement.

A large gray mop shifted forward into the light.

They could see the grime of a thousand dirty floors across her face.

"I am Mother Mop XII, queen of the cleaning supplies," the mop said. "What is this favor you ask?"

"We need to borrow a bucket," Scoop said. "We need to help Baron von Lineal—"

"Lineal sent you?" Mother Mop said.

"He did," Totz said. "We need to help everyone in the school."

"I owe Baron von Lineal a great many things," Mother Mop said. "The Main Office orders new ammonia when we need it. The Main Office sends us new paper towels when we are running low. And when it's time for me to step down as Queen Mother Mop XII, it is the Main Office who will send us Queen Mother Mop XIII. It is said she will come wrapped in plastic, just how I arrived so long ago."

Slice, Totz, and Scoop glanced at one another.

"So, may we borrow a bucket?" Slice asked.

Mother Mop nodded. "You may borrow a bucket, but you must return it, clean and un-damaged, before the end of the night."

"Well, that was easier than I thought," Scoop whispered.

A bucket tumbled out of the closet.

"Just come a bit closer to get it…" Mother Mop said.

They reached for the bucket, but the crunchy coating on Totz's arms prickled. He grabbed Slice and Scoop and pulled them aside. A broom slapped down on the tile right where they had been standing.

Suddenly, an army of cleaning supplies burst out of the closet.

"Baron von Lineal will *never* replace me," Mother Mop said as buckets, rags, and spray bottles charged out of the darkness. "I am Queen Mother Mop XII, and I will swab this school forever. Plus, you *are* food . . . and you *are* on the floor."

Slice, Scoop, and Totz grabbed the bucket, and they ran for their lives.

CHAPTER 9
It Must Be Mustard

They might have run down every hallway in Belching Walrus Elementary, but after ducking into the Tech Room, hiding under a desk in the Main Office, and jumping off the stage in the Auditorium, Slice, Scoop, and Totz finally escaped the cleaning supplies and made it back to the Cafeteria with the items they needed.

With the help of his friends, Slice set to work.

He filled the bucket with wood glue, dumped in some yellow paint, stirred it with a drumstick, and stuck a white label on the side of the bucket.

"What are we doing?" Totz asked.

"Just give me a second," Slice said. He took a black marker and began writing on the label. "Now, help me push this into the Pantry."

Totz and Scoop understood. They shoved the bucket until it started sliding across the floor. Finally, they wedged it against the wall next to the box of mustard packets.

"Maybe if Lauren eats this instead of one of the mustard packets, she won't get supercharged," Slice said.

"And maybe they'll finally go home," Totz said.

Scoop looked it over. "Something is wrong here," she said.

"Something is *definitely* wrong," a voice boomed behind them.

They spun around. It was Richard the dictionary with Spex Bifocals at his side.

"We're sorry," Scoop said. "But Gleb and Lauren have been cheating. They've been attacking innocent mustard packets. They've been—"

"Silence!" Spex said.

"Silence?" Totz muttered. "This isn't the Library."

Richard took the marker from Slice and set to work. He crossed out a few letters, added another, and inserted a few more.

"There," Richard said.

"Your ruse would never work with a poorly written label," Spex said. "Correct spelling is requisite."

"Ruse?" Totz said.

"Requisite?" Scoop said.

"Spelling?" Slice said.

SOMEONE WHO SPELLS POORLY IS CALLED A CACOGRAPHER.

Slice felt a tug on his crust. It was a mustard packet named Squirt.

"What can we do?" Squirt said. "We want to help, too."

Slice knelt down. "The best way to help is to find

a hiding spot," he said. "Find a hiding spot, and don't come out until I say it's safe."

Squirt planted her fists on her hips and nodded. "Understood," she said.

Trumpets blared from the Cafeteria.

Scoop tapped Slice on the shoulder. "The final event," she said. "We'd better get out there."

"What *is* the final event?" Totz asked.

Slice smiled. "Something very, very difficult," he said.

By the time everyone assembled, Baron von Lineal was already standing on his milk crate. "To all the folks at Belching Walrus Elementary," he announced.

"And planet Xyzyx!" Gleb called out. Lauren stood next to him with so many gold medals around her neck her face was barely visible.

"And planet Xyzyx," Baron von Lineal went on. "These Interdepartmental, Interdisciplinary,

Intergalactic Olympic Games have been very inter-esting and . . . educational. I believe in light of what has been happening, we can all agree it's time to be done with them."

"Hold on!" Scoop called out. She ran up the cen-ter aisle, climbed onto the milk crate, and whispered into Baron von Lineal's ear.

Baron von Lineal stood tall and cleared his throat. "It appears we have one last event," he said.

Scoop whispered in his ear some more.

"And the final event in our Inter—blah, blah, blah—Olympic Games is . . ." Baron von Lineal smiled. "The Deadly Dishwasher Obstacle Course!"

A gasp spread through the Cafeteria, followed by murmurs.

"Well, I guess we'll have to finish these Olympics winning one more event," Gleb said. "How many gold medals will that make, Lauren?"

"Squ@rk!" Lauren said.

"Exactly!" Gleb said. "So, who will be racing against Lauren?"

Not a single room in Belching Walrus Elementary wanted to take part in the Deadly Dishwasher Obstacle Course.

Baton from the Music Room declined for the instruments.

Chip from the Tech Room powered down.

Coach from the Gym forfeited.

Spex from the Library pulled them out of circulation.

Pineapple from the Cafeteria . . .

But it wouldn't be Pineapple running in the Deadly Dishwasher Obstacle Course that day. It would be Totz.

CHAPTER 10
The Deadly Dishwasher Obstacle Course

Totz listened to music on his headphones. It always helped him concentrate. Slice massaged Totz's shoulders while Scoop laid out the game plan.

"Okay, you know that dishwasher inside and out," she said. "That's your advantage. You'll have to dodge and flip and spin."

"Then you'll have to slide, jump, and limbo," Slice said.

"And then you'll have to shimmy, shake, and do the Worm," Scoop added.

A look of worry crossed their faces.

"And then I'll have to do a cartwheel," Totz said. "Uh . . . no problem."

But they all knew *no problem* didn't mean there was no problem. They all knew *no problem* was actually code for *Hey, y'all, we've got a big problem. I can't get through the Deadly Dishwasher Obstacle Course without doing a cartwheel, and tater tots can't do cartwheels. Maybe someone else should do it, or maybe we should call the whole thing off, or maybe I should run back into the Cooler and hide in the big box with all the other tater tots.*

Slice saw the worry on his friend's face. "I'll go," he offered. "I'll do the obstacle course."

"I appreciate it, dude," Totz said. "But I've got this."

Lauren was already standing at the mouth of the giant dishwasher stretching her tentacles.

Crowds had gathered.

The Tech Room had set up a large monitor and cameras so everyone on the outside of the dishwasher could see what was happening on the inside.

The Art Room was selling T-shirts.

The Music Room played a peppy tune.

Baron von Lineal stood on his milk crate. "It is time for the final event in the first ever Interdepartmental, Interdisciplinary, Intergalactic Olympic Games!"

The crowd cheered.

"It is a dangerous event," he went on. "The dishwasher is a place of legend. It is a place that strikes fear into even the toughest pieces of Salisbury steak. No morsel of food has ever entered the dishwasher and returned."

The dishwasher groaned and made a belching sound. Bubbles frothed from its mouth.

"I mean it," Slice said to Totz. "Just say the word and I'll go."

Totz shook out his tiny arms. "I know you would," he said. "But I've got this."

"Seriously," Scoop said. "It's the *dishwasher* . . ."

Totz grinned. "I've been training for this moment my entire life."

"It's only been a day or so," Slice said.

A DAY OR SO IS A LONG ⟷ TIME FOR A TATER TOT!!!

Suddenly, Gleb ran from the Pantry holding a tiny spoon. The spoon had a glistening yellow glob on it. Lauren gulped it down, but instead of saying her usual "Squ@rk!" this time it came out "Squ&rk?"

A look of worry crossed Gleb's face. "Er, maybe we could do this event tomorrow?" he said.

"Squ&rk," Lauren agreed.

"Nonsense," Baron von Lineal said. "We have a tight schedule to keep."

"Closing ceremonies start in thirteen minutes," Glizzy added.

"But what about the slam dunk contest?" Pineapple asked.

Everyone ignored Pineapple.

"Athletes, please go to the starting line," Coach announced. "You will begin on my tweet."

Totz and Lauren stepped onto the conveyor belt. As they got closer, Totz could smell decaying food and dirty dishwater.

Totz gulped.

He took a deep breath and went over the plan in his mind for the thousandth time.

He knew what to do.

At least he thought he knew what to do.

A red light started blinking on the dishwasher. A warning buzzer blared. The conveyor belt started drawing them in.

Lauren's stomach made a loud, gurgling sound.

"On your marks!" Baron von Lineal hollered. "Get set . . . !"

Coach tweeted.

Totz and Lauren bolted into the dishwasher.

The first moves were for the Wash Cycle. Dodge. Flip. Spin.

Totz dodged a blast of water from the right. He flipped over a blast of water from the left. Then he spun to avoid a jet of soapy suds. If he understood the plan correctly, he'd have to do that two more times.

Totz dodged, flipped, and spun as though his life depended on it (which he was pretty sure it did). Not a single drop of water or a single bubble of soap touched his crunchy and delicious outer layer.

He glanced back to see Lauren dodging, flip-ping, and spinning as well. She really was quite a good athlete. But there was no time to admire her skills. He had to concentrate.

KIDS, NEVER GO INTO A DISHWASHER WITHOUT PARENTAL SUPERVISION!!!

ACTUALLY, NEVER GO INTO A DISHWASHER AT ALL!

Over the growling of the dishwasher, Totz could hear the roar of the crowd. It gave him a boost and pushed him harder.

The next step was the Rinse Cycle. He needed to slide, jump, and then do the limbo. Twice.

Jets of water pulsed from the sides. Totz slid under the first jet, sprung to his feet, and jumped over the second. As the third jet of water came, he bent back as far as he could and limboed underneath the blast.

Lauren matched him move for move, but on the second limbo, the water jet clipped her shoulder.

"Squ@rk!" she cried out.

Outside, everyone gazed up at the monitors. A gasp spread through the crowd as Lauren SQU@RKED.

The next step was the Dry Cycle. Totz had to shimmy, then shake, then do the Worm.

He waggled his body left and right, then shook up and down as blasts of hot air puffed past him. He dropped to the ground and did the Worm as hard

as he could. His body pulsed forward along the conveyor belt as mechanical arms swung just above his shoulders.

A "Squ@rk!" sounded from behind him. Totz spun around to see Lauren get blasted by a puff of hot air. It blew her back, and she got hit again.

"SQU@RK!!!"

Lauren stumbled back, and a mechanical arm flattened her.

"SQU@RK!!! SQU@RK!!!"

Lauren's eyes were sunken, and her tentacles

seemed less beefy. She wasn't as fast or as strong as usual, and Totz worried she might get hurt. It was one thing to stop the aliens from planet Xyzyx from eating all the mustard packets; it was an entirely different matter to stand by and watch Lauren suffer.

He had to help.

CHAPTER 11

Totz to the Rescue!

Totz knew how to get through the dishwasher from beginning to end, but he had never thought about going from end to beginning. He needed to come up with a plan.

The blasts of air were coming from both sides: left, right, left, right. Something about the rhythm seemed familiar. Left, right, left, right. Then he remembered. Totz balled up his tiny fists and started speed-walking back to Lauren. Left, right, left, right. One foot on the ground at all times. Front leg straight when it hits the ground. Leg straight as it passes under your body.

It took a few steps to get the hang of it, but before long Totz's starchy hips were making the same strange figure-eight pattern Sal's and Monella's had. And with each twist, the blast of air shot past him. Left, right, left, right!

"Sal! Monella!" he cried out. "You've saved the day again!"

Totz speed-walked back and grabbed Lauren by a tentacle. "I've got you!" he hollered over the roar of the dishwasher. "We'll get out of here no problem!"

"Squ@rk!"

But Totz's words seemed to enrage the dishwasher. Jets sprayed harder. Air puffed more violently. Bubbles bubbled more bubbily.

Totz tried to shimmy and shake, but with Lauren at his side, the air puffs batted them around.

"Drop and do the Worm!" Totz yelled.

He and Lauren dropped to their bellies and started wiggling. Fortunately, when your body is half tentacles, it's not hard to learn a dance called *the Worm.*

Totz and Lauren wormed their way to the next chamber. It was filled with mechanical arms that swung this way and that.

"It's the Plate-Stacking Cycle," Totz said. "We have to do a cartwheel."

"Squ@rk!" Lauren replied.

Totz stepped forward, but Lauren held him back.

"Squ@rk!" she said, motioning to his arms.

"I know my arms are too short," Totz said. "But I have to try."

Lauren pointed to Totz and then to her belly. "Squ@rk!"

"No, you do not have permission to eat me," Totz said.

"Squ@rk!" Lauren said, shaking her head. Her tentacles slithered out and grabbed Totz. "Squ@rk!"

He wrapped his arms around her waist, and Lauren leaped sideways. Her tentacles splayed out like spokes of a wheel. It was the perfect cartwheel!

Mechanical arms swung up, down, back and forth, but not a single one touched them. Finally, they tumbled out of the back of the dishwasher to the roaring cheers of thousands. Totz stood up but fell back down as his friends rushed over.

"Are you okay?" Scoop asked him.

Totz looked up at them.

"Am I ... am I still crunchy and delicious?" Totz asked.

"Crunchy and delicious as ever," Slice said.

They picked him up and carried him on their shoulders. The crowd went wild.

Baron von Lineal climbed onto his milk crate.

"The winner of the Deadly Dishwasher Obstacle Course is . . ." The crowd hushed. "Well, it's a tie."

"A tie?" Slice called out. "Totz dominated in that dishwasher. We all saw it on the monitors!"

"I'd like to see Totz win a gold medal as much as anyone," Baron von Lineal said, "but they both came out of the dishwasher at the same time. By the rules of the Interdepartmental, In-  terdisciplinary, Intergalactic Olympic Games, this contest ends as a tie. Totz and Lauren will split the gold medal."

Boos echoed through the Cafeteria. But Totz climbed the milk crate and stood next to Baron von Lineal.

"I worked hard to win that event," he said. "But I never would have finished without Lauren's help. Tater tots just can't do cartwheels."

Gleb helped Lauren to her feet. He tried to feed her a spoonful of glistening yellow goop, but she pushed it away.

Totz cleared his throat. "And since I would never have finished on my own, Lauren from planet Xyzyx should win the gold medal. I will take silver."

Gleb's hands shot into the air. "YES!" he cried out.

"Thank you one and all for having us here," Gleb said, snatching the medal out of Baron von Lineal's hands. "We'll be going now. It was nice knowing you."

"Wait five billion nanoseconds," Chip said. "We have the whole race on video. We believe you should have a closer look at the finish line."

All eyes turned to the monitors as Chip sped through video footage from the obstacle course.

"Wow, I look pretty good," Totz said.

"You look like a deep-fried ninja," Scoop said.

"Your speed-walking technique could use some work," Sal said.

"But not bad for a first try," Monella added.

Finally, Chip slowed the video. `"It is the image of the finish line that is important,"` he explained as he hit pause on the tiny remote.

"Not only is it a fact that Totz's hand crossed the finish line first . . ." Chip explained. "But . . ."

"His hand touched the ground," Slice said.

"Totz did a cartwheel!" Scoop cried out.

Totz tiny arms shot into the air.

"Then it's settled," Baron von Lineal said. "For the Deadly Dishwasher Obstacle Course, Totz wins the gold!"

CHAPTER 12

Escape Is Im-pasta-ble

Everyone cheered. Well, everyone cheered except Gleb and Lauren. They were busy rushing up the ramp into their spaceship. Nearby, an empty bucket had been cast aside. Glistening yellow goop was splattered on the floor.

"Too late," Gleb said over his shoulder. "Lauren already won the gold medal. Now, we must be going. We've got a long trip back to planet Xyzyx."

The spaceship blinked red . . . blue . . . green . . .
red . . . blue . . . green . . .

"There's no yellow," Scoop said.

"Huh?" Slice asked.

"Their ship used to blink red, blue, green, *yellow*,"
she said. "Now it's only blinking red, blue, green.
Something is wrong."

The ramp to the spaceship closed, and the ship's lights glowed more brightly. The ship rose from the cafeteria table, sputtered, and then floated back down. It rose again. This time, the ship made a gushing sound and landed heavily. Steam puffed out. The ramp lowered, and Gleb and Lauren walked out.

"Squ@rk!" Lauren said.

"Lauren is correct," Gleb said, heading toward the Pantry. "It seems our ship is damaged. We'll just fix it up and be on our way. We just need a few supplies."

"Wait one second," Slice said. "What *sort* of supplies?"

"Squ@rk!" Lauren said. But this *Squ@rk!* sounded a little worried.

"Just . . . uh . . . a few . . . uh . . . a few supplies," Gleb sputtered. "You know, this and that."

"This and that?" Scoop said. "They've been stealing mustard packets!"

"Squ@rk!" Lauren said again.

"He's right," Totz said. "It's how Lauren won all the events. Mustard gives them strength, speed, and stamina."

"It gives them superpowers!" Slice said.

A look of anger crossed Gleb's face, but then he softened. "It's true," Gleb admitted. "Our spaceship blinks red, blue, green, and yellow for a reason. The red represents heat—the heat we need to work our fusion reactors. The blue represents water—the water we need to cool the cyber coils."

"Squ@rk!" Lauren said.

"Yes," Gleb said. "The cyber coils do get quite hot during intergalactic travel."

"The *g* in *green* stands for *gold* . . . we need the gold medals. Gold is our main source of fuel. It's dense with golden goodness, and it's why we travel the universe winning competitions."

"So, the yellow represents mustard," Slice said.

Gleb nodded. "Mustard is the most valuable substance on planet Xyzyx. It powers the computers on our ship. It gives us strength and speed. We cannot survive without it."

"But some of my closest friends are mustard," Glizzy said. "What's a hot dog without mustard?"

"But if we don't get mustard, we'll starve," Gleb

explained. "And we won't be able to power our computers."

"I'm terribly sorry," Baron von Lineal said. "You may have won all those gold medals, but we cannot allow you to take any more mustard packets."

Gleb and Lauren ran into the Pantry. By the time anyone else got there, the aliens were already dumping boxes and overturning crates

to find the mustard packets. Slice could see the mustard packets on the very top shelf. Squirt was peeking her head out of a box of pasta.

He motioned for her to hide.

But it was too late. Gleb had seen Squirt and started climbing. Lauren trailed right behind him. In seconds, they were halfway up the shelving.

"There's no way we'll catch them in time," Scoop said.

Totz climbed onto the lowest shelf. "All the speed walking in the world won't get us up there," he said.

Suddenly, something crashed behind them. It was Pineapple! He was running toward the shelves.

"SLAM DUNK TIME!" he called out.

Pineapple leaped into the air. He soared over everyone's heads up to the second, the third, the fourth shelf. He grabbed one of Gleb's tentacles with one hand and one of Lauren's with the other. As he fell back down, Lauren and Gleb tried to hold on, but

Pineapple was too heavy. They all landed in a heap on the floor.

When the dust settled, Gleb and Lauren were pinned under Pineapple.

"What are we supposed to do?" Gleb said. "We *need* mustard."

"It is far worse than that," BLU1 the drone said. "During the games, GRN1

and I plugged into their ship. Gleb and Lauren have been traveling from planet to planet."

GRN1 continued: "They devour all the mustard until there is none left. Then they move on to seek out more."

"A planet without mustard . . ." Glizzy said. "It would be a wasteland."

"Squ@rk!!" Lauren said.

"We only stopped them because we made fake mustard out of glue and yellow paint," Scoop said.

"It took help from just about every room at the school, but we got it done," Totz said.

"You know," Slice said, looking back and forth between the dishwasher and Gleb's spaceship. "I think I have an idea . . . Pineapple, Ducky, Apple, Bass Drum, Richard the dictionary . . . Come with me. We need all the muscle we can get."

Totz knew what Slice had in mind. "Chip," he said. "Gather your folks, too. We may need some tech support."

Slice admired their handiwork. "It wasn't easy, but we did it," he said.

"It's a brilliant solution," Scoop said.

"Gleb and Lauren can live in the mouth of the dishwasher," Totz explained. "They can eat any food that comes in and no one will ever know."

"Squ@rk!" Lauren called out from the dishwasher. Her eyes were less sunken, and her tentacles were more beefy than before.

Gleb walked to the edge of the conveyor belt. "Thank you, one and all," he said. "If it weren't for the folks at Belching Walrus Elementary, Lauren and I would still be roving around the universe pillaging planet after planet of their precious mustard. Now we have a place we can call home."

139

Cheers rose up from the crowds, and the closing ceremonies began.

BLU1, GRN1, and a squadron of other drones flew over. An army of balls bounced across the room. Trumpets blared and drums pounded. Jets of different-colored paint squirted into the air. Confetti glittered above them.

Slice, Scoop, and Totz had had enough excitement for one night. They hung out in their usual place at the base of the utility sink and watched from a distance. Friends, both old and new, joined them.

"An entire Interdepartmental, Interdisciplinary, Intergalactic Olympic Games all in one night," Slice said.

"Plus, stopping an alien abduction," Scoop said.

"And getting through the dishwasher in one piece," Totz added.

"And saving all us mustard packets!" Squirt said.

"And discovering the value of speed walking," Sal said.

"Squ@rk!" Lauren added.

"Exactly what I was thinking," Slice said. "Squ@rk."

"By the way," Scoop asked Slice. "What was the one favor you asked of Baron von Lineal?"

"Not much," Slice said. "Just something for a friend."

**Keep reading for a sneak peek of the first book
from the Bad Food Club!**

Game of Scones

CHAPTER 1
The Way It's Always Bean

In many ways, Belching Walrus Elementary is probably similar to your school. There is a flagpole with a flappy flag in front. There are big heavy doors that slam shut when you walk in. There are hallways that lead to different classrooms. There is an auditorium with a stage, a gymnasium with sports equipment, and a library with books. There is a cafeteria where the food lives. And, just like in

your school, after all the doors are locked, the food
in the cafeteria comes alive to party.

What's that, you say? The food in your cafeteria *doesn't* come alive each night to party? Well, next time you get a chance, grab your sleeping bag and a flashlight and camp out under one of the lunch tables for the evening. You'll see.

Note: When you do camp out in your school's cafeteria, be sure to bring your own food. Not only is eating the food from your cafeteria without paying for it stealing, but the food will run away before you have a chance to pop it in your mouth.

So before you read any further, you should get to know some of the folks who live at Belching Walrus Elementary. I mean, if you don't like our characters, you might not want to read on. You might want to toss this book over your shoulder and move on to something more your speed. Bench-pressing kittens? Snowshoeing through the Alps with a yeti? Skydiving with a silverback gorilla? Hey, whatever browns your toast.

Slice

Food Type: Slice of pizza

Flavor: Cheesy

Personality: Chipper and always positive

Strengths: Boundless energy, ultra-friendly

Weaknesses: Fear of the microwave (it makes him soggy) and mice (they like cheese)

Hobbies: He's not sure . . .

Scoop

Food Type: Triple scoop ice cream cone

Flavor: Vanilla, chocolate, and strawberry

Personality: Super sweet, but also super focused

Strengths: Planning and strategy

Weaknesses: Can be melty at times

Catchphrase: "That's driptastic!" (Actually, she never
   says that. It's silly.)

Hobbies: Painting and graffiti

Totz

Food Type: Tater tot (don't call him a "Potato Puff"—that's what they call his granddad)

Flavor: Delicious!

Personality: Laid-back, but trendy

Strengths: Spitting mad rhymes

Weaknesses: Fear of the deep fryer, fear of public speaking

Hobbies: Spoken-word poetry

Of course, there are plenty of other folks in the Belching Walrus Elementary Cafeteria—baskets filled with fruits, a huge jar of pickles, a Cooler filled with chocolate milks and apple juices, and a freezer filled with ice pops and yet-to-be-nuked chicken nugs—but you'll learn about them as the story

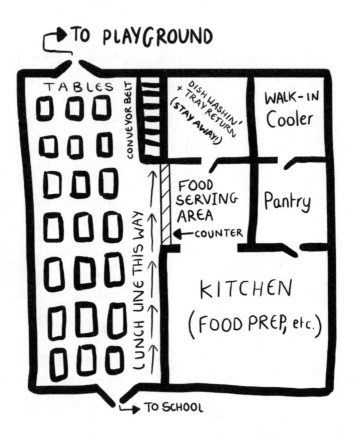

unfolds. Right now, just know that Slice, Scoop, and Totz, as usual, were hanging out under the lunchroom sink.

And not one of them knew their perfect lives were about to change forever.